Practice

Judith Namala
A Novella

Serubiri Moses

Center for Art,
Research and Alliances

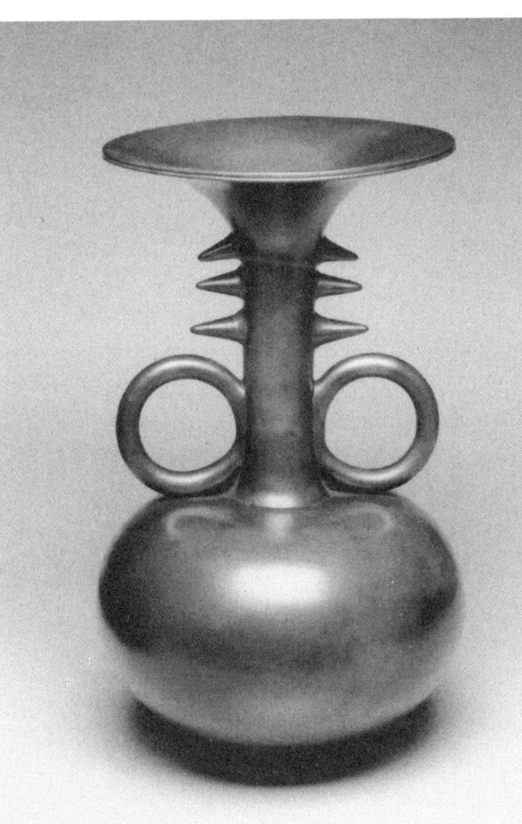

Magdalene Anyango N. Odundo,
Symmetrical Reduced Black Narrow-Necked Tall Piece, 1990
Terracotta, 16 × 10 × 10 in.
Brooklyn Museum, New York

Preface

Masaka 1980s

Masaka, a town ten miles from the small village where Judith Namala was born and raised, was located about fifty miles north of the Uganda-Tanzania border town of Mutukula. It was less than ten miles west of Lake Victoria, formerly Lake Nalubaale, so named for the deities in the Buganda cosmology. The larger Masaka District stood south of the Buganda kingdom—near the center of Uganda—and was one of its major gombololas, or administrative centers. The Buganda clan system and its various institutions, founded more than five centuries ago, stretched all the way from Kampala in the west, to the shores and islands of Lake Victoria in the east, and to the border of Tanzania in the south. Because the colonists came from the east, arriving from the eastern coast via port cities like Mombasa and Zanzibar, Kampala functioned as the second hub to Jinja, an industrial town on the fringes of Buganda, about seventy miles east toward Kenya. Kampala was now considered the administrative, political, and cultural capital of Uganda, but there were other native administrative centers across the country, including Fort Portal, a seat of Toro, and Gulu, about two hundred miles north of Kampala, which was the seat of Acholiland.

Ntinda-Kiwatule 1999

If you jumped on a boda ridden by one of those former child soldiers or kadogos like Juma, who happened to father Judith Namala's child Subira, you rode down Kampala Road for less than five miles toward the east. At the Nakawa-Ntinda junction there was a turn to your left. You told the boda driver not to turn at the Makerere Business School, but further along opposite the Mercedes-Benz warehouse. You went along this Ntinda Road for less than five miles, until you arrived in a district called Ntinda-Kiwatule. The area had a history: It was not developed as part of the capital city's urban plan, designed by German architect Ernst May in the 1940s; it bordered, to one side, the Nakawa African settlement, built for African workers in the city, and to the other, Naguru, a planned white suburb. Ntinda-Kiwatule was not an affluent white borough, and while it did not have the status of a college town, it had the feeling of one: The professors who taught at the Business School lived close by in Ntinda, and those who owned the 1940s May-designed homes in the African resettlement of Nakawa spilled over and bought land in the surrounding area of Ntinda-Kiwatule. What one would find there were relatively modest shops and restaurants and a mushrooming of red roof tile bungalows across a hilly expanse of no more than ten square miles. Esther Nambi and Geoffrey Opolot lived here, in relative peace and quiet. Their red brick bungalow was surrounded by friendly neighbors associated with the British colonial schools: Kisubi, Gayaza, Namagunga, and Buddo. This was the native elite.

I

Ntinda-Kiwatule 1993

These lazy maids! Esther Nambi cursed. The madam woke up this morning and her husband, Geoffrey Opolot, had already gone to work. These were the gendered roles of factory labor: He went to one factory, and she stayed at another. Except most people did not say that the factory at home supported the other factory to which all the men went off for the day. Who fed them? Bathed them? Clothed them? Cleaned the sweat off their backs? That morning, the live-in maid, Judith Namala, did not alert the madam that her husband had already gotten out of bed and hastily left the house to go to work. The madam was bitter now, because her husband, Geoffrey Opolot, drove to work that morning having spoiled the child's doll. *What will baby Martha do without her doll? These lazy maids!* she cursed. *Martha will cry all day long and disturb me.*

II

Ntinda-Kiwatule 1993

Some say that the coming of a maid is a ritual. That the family waits patiently in the living room to inspect the maid. Others say that the maid arrives unannounced and without pretext. The house produces maids. As in a factory, the home easily finds its division of labor, its factory workers and supervisors. In the factory, she will become part of the family album.

When Judith Namala arrived at Esther Nambi and Geoffrey Opolot's three-bedroomed house in Ntinda-Kiwatule, they were not expecting the kind of meticulously dressed woman who walked in that early evening. With a model's face, she appeared like Diouana, a character invented by Ousmane Sembène and interpreted by Mbissine Thérèse Diop: a black girl sauntering elegantly into her white madam's house.

Judith Namala wore her hair in neat cornrows, which she partially covered over with a silk headscarf. No one would have guessed she had beauty and style. She wore a long floor-length maxi skirt and a bright pink flowing blouse. Judith Namala walked into the house at night rather than during the day because, as per this household's ritual, both the husband and wife were to be present upon the maid's arrival.

Judith Namala sat down in a manner that proved that she was raised by parents in a proper home and not like a malnourished dog feeding on a rubbish heap. The way to kneel in Buganda, the ethnic society she came from, is to kneel without clumsily falling over to one side like a sack of sweet potatoes, without holding onto any support as you slowly descend to the floor. You should kneel with care and make a slight movement with the lowering of your eyes to acknowledge the presence of those to whom you would like to give respect. That first time, Judith Namala knelt without falling to either side. Her kneeling was refined. It was the mark of style and elán. Judith Namala sat neatly on the woven sisal mat without planting either of her forearms in a way that faces outward and shows the inside of the elbow, the cubital fossa. She sat for what seemed like an eternity. Her spine was as sharp as a needle. It was the act of a gymnast or competitive athlete. She was barely a woman and years later, when the family grew to see her as one of their own, the husband and wife's three children—Tendo, Martha, and Josiah—would call her, to the shock of Esther Nambi, their second mother. This was not the position of a second wife. Geoffrey Opolot and men like him feared being brought to trial for sleeping with the maid. When she appeared in the family album, a fact that raised mixed feelings in Judith Namala, she was photographed seated on the woven sisal mat, eating with the children, their cousin, and their cousin's maid. Her madam Esther Nambi would sit in the upholstered chair with the "real" mothers—the blood relatives. This distinction was emphasized. Motherhood was a part of her life while tending to the Opolot household. Though as an unmarried woman and maid, Judith Namala would be denied it.

III

Every maid is a reflection of her madam
Every maid is created by her madam's economic need

Every maid will become her madam
She will become the madam she swore never to become

When she grows up, a maid will leave her home
And go into the house of a stranger

Every circumstance in a maid's life will
bring her to this moment

Every maid wants to be *head of household*
Every maid dreams of taking over her master's house

IV

Ntinda-Kiwatule 1996

Judith Namala never joined a domestic workers' association (though domestic workers in Kampala did so in the late 1990s prior to her departure from her madam's house), nor did she directly address thc disparities of her employment. As a laywoman, Judith Namala knew little about the law. She was not the archetypal worker. She received some instruction at church, and then in her madam's house. This was her education. She was unlike Shamilla who, after her tenure as a domestic worker, became a sex worker and ascended into Kampala celebrity.

A madam is a married woman with a busy schedule. As a consultant, the madam's briefcase stands out. Because of her at-work schedule and briefcase, a madam is viewed by the maid as a man. The madam is self-aware: She knows that *having a maid is really about playing madam*, as the writer Zukiswa Wanner tells us. The madam is part of a play. Its main character shuttles between the various rooms of the home and the cultivated patch of land in her backyard. The maid is also a character in this play, though her role seems hidden. She is not at center stage. She is off-stage and occasionally haunts the set of the play. She makes the moral of the story. A Greek chorus.

A ghost rising up to haunt the home. Where the story takes a sudden turn.

V

Ntinda-Kiwatule 1993

It is seven in the morning. Ntinda-Kiwatule is already buzzing with people trying to get to work—you can hear the cars honking and swooshing by on the tarmac outside their home. Judith Namala has gotten the breakfast going and is setting the table. She prepares some millet porridge, as usual, with some African tea. The recipe is: milk, tea leaves, cinnamon sticks, ground cardamom, and ginger brought to a boil. She lays the table, gives the children their metal enamel cups, and places the porridge into metal enamel bowls. She brings out two flasks (one for porridge and one for tea) and she places them on the table for Geoffrey Opolot and madam Esther to serve themselves. The breakfast is complemented by escorts, a colloquial term: steamed muwogo, or cassava; lumonde, or sweet potato; Tip Top bread, and Blue Band margarine. The children, Tendo and Josiah, rush to the table and spread their Tip Top white bread slices with margarine. Judith Namala sits down on a sisal mat laid on the floor next to the table. She holds baby Martha and feeds her with a bottle. The entire family eats in silence. Then all at once Geoffrey Opolot declares: *Saawa ya kola!*

VI

Ntinda-Kiwatule 1993

When Judith Namala had retired from doing house chores in the late afternoon, and sometimes in the early evening, she would go outside to smoke taaba—tobacco leaves wrapped in thin paper. The house had an area for smoking in the backyard, next to the small patch of land on which Esther Nambi would keep her fruit-bearing matooke, or green bananas, as well as her yams (she had a variety, including a rare white yam called balugu), ebijanjaalo (beans, a staple), and muwogo. It was a tradition: As soon as a young woman entered into her own home, she would secure a patch of land to grow food.

Esther Nambi had married Geofrey Opolot at the start of 1990, just before Nelson Mandela was released from prison. Relatives would warn her to care for her garden by clearing the kikolo, or banana root, and by covering over any roots with dried leaves so as not to provoke the curiosity and ire of witches who would take advantage and leave hostile spirits in her garden.

We do not know for certain whether the maid Judith Namala had something to do with these hostile spirits. Though a country girl, and an unmarried woman, Judith Namala took up smoking once she arrived in the city. It was a habit she had first picked up in her teen years during the '80s, having been raised by a grandmother who smoked taaba herself. Now, she could be seen, religiously, in the small patch of land near the clothesline at the back of the house, smoking taaba every night.

The three-bedroomed house had one back door that led to the yard and garden patch, which was surrounded by a chain-link fence. The kitchen greeted everyone from the front. It was as though the architect had wanted the entire family to enter the house through the kitchen, an unusual design decision that went against convention. A parlor room usually came first, facing the front and welcoming guests.

In the madam's house, one room was for the children (where the maid also slept), and another for Esther Nambi and Geoffrey Opolot. The third was a guest bedroom. Like most of the houses in the Ntinda-Kiwatule area, Esther Nambi's house was made of short red clay bricks that decorated the wall. Wooden beams in a raised ceiling made the house cool on hot days. The veranda had short, white concrete columns, colloquially called pompeii, a reference to classical Greco-Roman building. Like most homes, this building had a gate that was larger than life. The gate, along with the high-walled fences, was called e'kikomera, an enclosure with the connotation of a prison. The gate alone spanned three meters and had spikes at the top. When Geoffrey Opolot honked his horn at the gate, Judith Namala opened the metal doors outward. Geoffrey Opolot would not smile at her, as it was said: Smiling at the maid was a sign of malintent.

VII

Women like Esther Nambi, despite their British educations, were often inclined to grow a garden of food on their small patches of land. If a young woman did not grow food, she was often looked down upon. In her home, Esther Nambi would grow the fruit-bearing matooke plant, rather than the mbidde plant, which did not bear fruit. The mbidde was auspicious. It could be found in a small patch belonging to a home occupied by a father of twins. It brought wealth to this man. Esther Nambi's people nurtured the diversity of the banana plants. In another part of the world, only one or two types of fruit-bearing banana plants were grown. Had Esther Nambi been a bit more adventurous she could have grown gonja, or plantain, in the small garden patch behind her house in Ntinda-Kiwatule. She could have grown ndiizi, a smaller kind of yellow banana. But Esther Nambi did not take many risks in her garden patch. As her relatives had warned, one had to exercise extreme caution to avoid the ire of witches, especially if the witch was a family member, or worse, a live-in maid. If you left your plants untended—the dried banana leaves and uprooted roots and cut stems strewn about in a disorderly manner—this family member or the maid herself came round and did with the roots and stems what they liked. You would no doubt receive what you were looking for. Witches came to your garden and performed rituals with these discarded parts, as if to teach you a lesson in tending to your garden. It was a lesson for which you paid dearly.

VIII

Ntinda-Kiwatule 1993

In the kitchen, Esther Nambi shows Judith Namala the various electrical appliances. While Judith Namala indeed came from Masaka town, she at the very least knew how to operate basic electric appliances. *This is called a juicer. We use it to make juice. Now, watch me and let me show you how to use it. Firstly, wash these mangoes and passion fruits.* Esther Nambi said this, pointing to a heap of fruit on the kitchen top. *Secondly, peel and cut the mangoes into small cubes and cut open the passion fruit and scoop out the juicy seeds. Thirdly, empty the peeled fruit into the juicer and switch it on like so.* Esther Nambi turned on the juicer, which immediately made a loud screeching noise. Judith Namala, having never heard the sound of a juicer before, jumped up in terror: *Mama nyabo!* she cried out. *Miss mother!* She ran out the kitchen door holding up her skirt so she wouldn't trip and fall on her way out. It was just like an episode of the television series *That's Life Mwattu!*, in which the character of Nakawunde, the second wife–having arrived from the village–stumbles, and eventually settles into city life. She clumsily performs the chores of a live-in maid, distracted from her work by the radio; she has gotten in trouble yet again. Nakawunde had come to be synonymous with the image of the rural woman maid. Esther Nambi laughed out loud.

She said: *ekyaalo kijja ku kugwaamu.* Soon the village will leave your body.

Whenever this was said, it was not meant as a compliment. It was worse than: *You speak good English.* It was said to remind whoever was addressed that they were closer to barbarism than civilization. If they were not careful, they would easily slip back. It was as if Esther Nambi did not know the saying "You can take me out of the hood but you can't take the hood out of me." Or the English idiom: "Once a villager, always a villager." Esther Nambi found Judith Namala hiding in the children's bedroom, where she slept on the lower deck of a three-decker bed and the children on the top two levels. Martha slept in her parent's bedroom. *Auntie Esther n'ekanze nnyo*, she said. (Judith Namala called Esther Nambi auntie, addressing her as the children did. This showed a kind of respect that revealed Esther Nambi was higher up in the household hierarchy than she was.) Judith Namala's terror was so intense that she was visibly sweating. Esther Nambi, by now, having realized that this was not comedy, told Judith Namala to calm down. The blender was incapable of murder. Soon enough, she would get used to the sound.

IX

The home is a factory. An itinerary for household work might include: (1) daily washing of the car from 6–6:30 am, because the roads are dusty in Kampala and the car will be covered in dirt each day; (2) preparing millet porridge and black or African tea (made with cinnamon, cardamom, and milk) for a family of five or more for breakfast; (3) ironing the school uniforms for the children (this is done between ages four and ten, after which the children can iron their own clothes); (4) mopping the house floors (often by hand); (5) doing the laundry (often by hand); (6) sweeping the yard (usually with a long broom); (7) preparing lunch (and packing it in heated flasks) and delivering the lunch to Geoffrey Opolot's office in Old Kampala; (8) returning home from a long commute to give the children lunch, if the live-in domestic worker has not picked them up from school; (9) taking dry clothes off the clothesline; (10) ironing bed sheets, ready for the madam to make her own bed, and making the children's beds; (11) serving dinner; (12) cleaning up after dinner; (13) guarding the home against thieves, thugs, or break-ins at night. Such a factory often requires four live-in domestic workers, including an askari, a house boy, a house girl, and a nanny.

X

Maid, houseboy, gardener, laborer. Kazi is Swahili for work. And mukozi, Luganda for worker. Because she often works for many years, if not decades, in one household, she or he can become part of the family–a sibling, aunt, uncle, or distant relative. There are benefits to joining the household as a child: of privileged birth or adoption. She will inherit clothing. The hand-me-downs that come from siblings, or parents, or aunts and uncles. She will receive medical care. But often, she will not. Often the maid is illiterate. In some cases, she or he will receive instruction in reading and writing. Often, she or he will travel a distance to work in the household. She is rural. She will not speak to the children in English. The children will remain children. She will become the children's second parent. The madam will oversee this factory.

XI

Masaka 1989

On her way to Kampala city from Masaka, Judith Namala would take the main highway connecting the Central region of Uganda to the south toward Tanzania. The journey was less than seventy-five miles and two hours long by taxi van imported from Japan. In the van, which traveled on the main highway of paved tarmacked roads as it sped out of town, Judith Namala thought about the child she had left back home. She had given birth to Subira two years before moving to Kampala. Since she wasn't married and there was no man to father and pay for the child's upkeep, Judith Namala had to leave her hometown, entrusting her mother with the care of Subira, and go to the city. A maternal aunt who already lived in the city told her about an opening for a live-in domestic worker in the neighborhood of Ntinda-Kiwatule, and she migrated. Once there and established, she could send monthly income to her mother for her child's expenses.

Subira's father, Juma, was a young man Judith met one day when roaming about a borehole with her girlfriend Cissy Nantume. The child came healthy, bouncing, overweight, and loud. She scared Judith Namala. She had brought this child into the world. What would she do now? The child needed to be vaccinated.

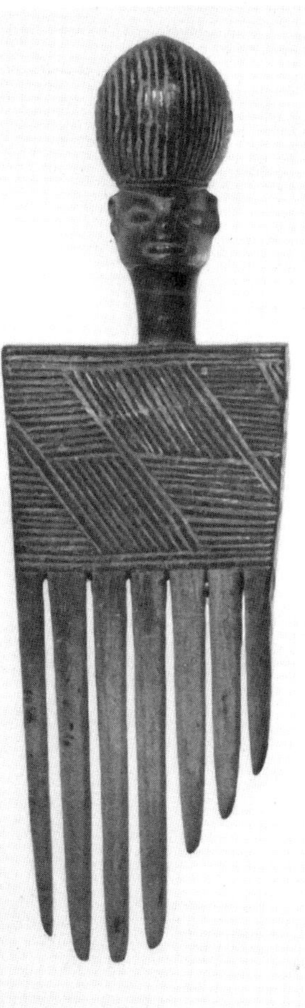

Chokwe, *Comb*, twentieth century
Wood, 6 × 1¾ × 1½ in.
Brooklyn Museum, New York

She needed clothes. Her mother taught her how to care for the child. How to feed the baby with her breast milk. Her grandmother prepared ekyogero to bathe the child in therapeutic herbs. After the ekyogero, the bath in which the child was washed regularly for a few months, the child was then taken to her father's side of the family. There, she would be named Subira by a wise elder. A word for hope or great expectation.

XII

Ntinda-Kiwatule 1993

Judith Namala could plait a magnificent braid of hair to rival the precision of algorithmic machines, or sweep the yard, manicure the lawn, and prune the overgrown bushes in Esther Nambi's garden to a degree of perfection that was unheard of. It is not that principles of beauty were alien to Judith Namala. Esther Nambi, of British-trained manners and refined taste, did not fail to take note. Her irritation and annoyance with Judith Namala's domestic abilities only grew.

XIII

Ntinda-Kiwatule 1993

Esther Nambi has a lunch meeting with her old girl Jessica Nansubuga from Gayaza high school (where they both took classes in home economics) at the Ekitoobero Restaurant on Nakasero Road, near the golf course in an affluent and leafy part of Kampala. Jessica Nansubuga is a lawyer and women's advocate with the National Women Lawyers Association, an organization deemed "deadly" and "menacing" by many men, particularly married men. Jessica Nansubuga recounted: *Ever since we won that divorce case in 1994 in which Nankya was granted her right to claim damages caused by her husband's negligence of their marriage—since then, men have been up in arms as their marriages come under the gavel in divorce court.* The waiter interrupted Jessica Nansubuga's monologue to deliver a mouthwatering platter of food to the table. The two old girls had ordered the best of the restaurant's signature menu: cow-hoof stew, greens, steamed green bananas, and dried fish in groundnut stew steamed in smoked banana leaves, accompanied by passion fruit juice.

After the meal, Esther Nambi exclaims, *emmere ya wano e'mpoomera ddala*, giving the restaurant its flowers. She feigns fullness, stretching her arms to the sky. To bring her back from her pleasure dream, Jessica Nansubuga asks: *How are things at home? Is Geoffrey well, and how are the children?* Esther Nambi begins: *All is well, they are all doing fine.* Then digresses to talk about Judith Namala: *I just hired a maid.* She said it in this way. Flat. Direct. She didn't twist words like toys in a child's hand. She didn't make it seem like the maid was brought to her or otherwise brought to the home by her husband (which was unlikely, as men did not hire maids). She showed no signs of guilt about playing madam; she needed a maid and hired one. *Judith arrived from Masaka one month ago*, she continued. Her face fell: *It's as if she didn't come from the village at all.* The breeze blew from the nearby golf course and ruffled the leaves of plants crowding around them.

Her report was clinical: *Judith is unusually clean for a Country Girl. She does the house chores on time, feeds the baby on time, burps her, and puts her to sleep perfectly. She kneels down for my husband Geoffrey.* Then she paused. *I am yet to make up my mind about Judith. She seems too good to be true.* Noticing Esther Nambi's envy of Judith Namala, Jessica Nansubuga knew immediately what to say, and what not to say. She agreed with Esther Nambi's assessment of her maid, commenting: *In fact, it is unlikely for maids like Judith, who come from the village, to be on time and not mess up once when given a task.*

The fact was that the urban middle-class wives were at a crossroads with their poor and rural housemaids. If it was acknowledged that every maid wanted to become her madam—and men openly wrote opinion pieces on the subject in the print daily—then the ascension of rural women into the urban working class would have to be acknowledged too. They had come one step closer to social nobility and success.

XIV

Ntinda-Kiwatule 1997

Judith Namala was a villager, and a rural-born maid, now working in Ntinda-Kiwatule. She was no different from other villagers or rural-born maids, this much was true. But there were maids born in Kampala, in city slums or less-affluent parts. Hiring madams weeded out Kampala-born maids, who were said not to easily conform. City-born maids were hard-headed, prone to complain or to strike. They quickly quit their jobs, leaving their employers stranded. You could teach a villager how to catch a fish, and she would gather a whole farm. But madams believed you couldn't teach a city-born maid how to fish. She could only learn so much before plotting an insurrection. Heads of household feared city-born maids the way white people feared the violent insurrection of enslaved Africans.

Yet, the Judith Namalas, who were in demand–partly due to their ability to conform to the rules of a particular household without her employers fearing retaliation–would not share the same benefits that their city-born colleagues did. Domestics worked for a single family for anywhere between five years and two decades if the household was stable enough. They passed multiple seasons in a particular home, attended weddings and funerals. Despite their position (which was cherished) they could not easily negotiate better wages, and thus maintained an economic position which would only moderately, but never significantly, increase during the long tenure of their employment. City-born maids, on the other hand, were more than likely to ask for fairer and higher wages, and once they had some grasp of the household tasks and home management as a vocation, they easily transitioned into other kinds of work. It was not unusual for a city-born maid to transition to restaurant or hotel work. The many small kafundas inKampala City were run by former housemaids; they formed a large part of the restaurant and food industry. Those who were more ambitious went into sex work. Of these latter, former city-born maids, it has been said that they could be seen driving around the city of Kampala in their black, white, or silver G- and M-class Mercedes-Benzes with custom number plates.

XV

Ntinda-Kiwatule 1997

Literate women (abasomi, as they are disparagingly called) like Esther Nambi and Jessica Nansubuga fought for their rights in courts of law, at their places of work, in parliament, on the home front. In women's associations and in cooperative savings banks. But they did not, as yet, see clearly the struggle of rural women like Judith Namala, who indeed had children of their own and, unlike their heads of household, only saw their children at Christmastime, when they returned to the village for a week. And the same was true of the Judith Namalas, who could not fathom that women with the amount of privilege that the Esther Nambis possessed could complain of anything at all.

Maids saw their madams as men, the novelist Jennifer Nansubuga Makumbi once said at a literature festival. But how could the maids see their madams as women? They did not kneel before their own husbands. They drove off to work and left the maids to nurse their babies to sleep. There was a lack of recognition. Master and servant had never looked each other in the eye, wrote the playwright Robert Serumaga. The servant did not know how tall the master was, and neither did the master know how tall the servant was.

XVI

Masaka 1988

Judith Namala and her friend Cissy Nantume sat on a mat in their home compound. It was 1988. Their small village was about ten kilometers outside of Masaka town. As they talked and laughed with each other, they sat in the way that Baganda women were trained to do. Backs straight as a needle, they knelt down gracefully, without planting their forearms on the ground for support as "lazy" girls and boys did. Hands in lap. Cissy Nantume said, with a surprised look on her face: *Yesterday, when I came back from fetching water at the well, I saw a boy called Juma, who had been assembling mud bricks at a workshop close by. He asked me to bring this to you.* Cissy Nantume looked down and unfolded carefully wrapped banana leaves to reveal a palmful of entuntunu, ground cherries. The small orange-yellow physalis fruits that looked like colored gumballs were a treat that Judith Namala had enjoyed since childhood. She was pleased. That was the start of her romance. And over the next few weeks she would go with Cissy Nantume whenever her friend was on her way to the well, herself pretending to fetch water, but eager to spend time speaking with Juma, the boy who sent her a palmful of ground cherries wrapped neatly in banana leaves.

XVII

Ntinda-Kiwatule 1993

Geoffrey Opolot was warming his Pajero Wagon, ready to leave for the day, when Martha started crying because her doll was spoiled. In a fit, Esther Nambi scolded her husband: *Look at what you've done! You ruined Martha's doll. Martha will cry all day. You can't even make time for me or Martha. Look at you leaving the house with Martha in tears. She will cry all day.* Geoffrey Opolot defended his leaving the house with Martha in tears, saying he was going to find bread and money. His role was breadwinner for the household. But Esther Nambi insisted that as the child's father, Geoffrey Opolot had a duty to quiet his daughter Martha, to calm her down, particularly now that he was to blame for spoiling her doll. Martha, reduced to tears, would cry all day, and disturb Esther Nambi. Geoffrey Opolot, incensed that his wife would reduce his role to quieting his daughter's crying, told her defiantly that he was the breadwinner and wouldn't do a damn thing about it, nor would he fix Martha's doll.

XVIII

Ntinda-Kiwatule 1993

There's a moment in early infancy when a child has matured enough to want an object. For many children, that object is a mirror. It is something like a doll–that is to say, it is another. When young girls, especially, want a doll, they carry the doll on their backs, and fondle the doll in their arms as if it were real. Outside of the city, the village girls are encouraged to carry a wooden or fiber doll, tying them with strings to their backs. Like those wooden dolls we now see displayed in glass cases at the Quai Branly. But it was rather simple. The doll was only a mirror. The doll was an other.

XIX

So, the doll cried, and when it did, just like those hard plastic dolls, its mother, now only a girl, comforted her. She held the doll in her arms as if she were capable of crying all day, forgetting perhaps that she herself was still only a girl, a child in fact, and believing that this object, this thing she held in her arms was real. And so the doll cried, and its girl-mother quieted it, and talked to it, sometimes worrying that she would cry all day and disturb her. The girl-mother worried about the doll and carried the doll on her back, and sang to the doll, and washed the doll in water, and bathed the doll and combed its hair. She was real. She had ceased to be plastic.

XX

On the day that Martha got her hard plastic doll, her mother worried that she was not yet in a position to carry it and look after it. Esther Nambi, who herself (as a girl) had been given by her mother one of those blue-eyed hard plastic dolls, with the flaxen white hair and matching blue dress, worried that her daughter was not yet ready for a doll. *Will she love her?* Esther Nambi asked herself as she went hand-in-hand with Martha to the shopping mall. Martha did not know what kind of plastic doll she would get that morning. All she knew was that her mother, the madam, had told her she would buy her a doll.

XXI

Ntinda-Kiwatule 1993

Judith Namala would call out to Martha to give her a cool drink of water or juice in the mid-morning before continuing her play with the plastic doll. But Martha was so absorbed in the combing of the synthetic hair and the changing of the plastic doll's tiny clothes that Judith Namala would have to go to find Martha in the garden, behind the house, so that she could personally drag her inside. Martha lost herself in the play. The mirror had become more than an object: It had become this girl-mother's entire world. There could be loud music playing in the street—usually a traveling sound-system placed atop a van or a truck advertising an upcoming Kadongo Kamu concert, "one man playing a guitar," the country's folk music. Martha didn't hear it.

XXII

Ntinda-Kiwatule 1999

At school, where the girls had practiced (and refined) the art of comparison, Martha would boast about the plastic doll, which her mother, the madam, did not allow her to bring to school. She boasted in front of the other girl-mothers, who told Martha that they too had their own plastic dolls at home. They debated who had the tallest doll, or whose doll had the best hair. They secretly brought some of the doll's accessories to school for evidence in these debates: little items of clothing like the blue and white striped pinafore dresses, and the tiny doll shoes and tiny doll purses.

XXIII

Ntinda-Kiwatule 1999

Esther Nambi's household rules: the toys must be placed back in their boxes, the bicycles must be put nicely in the garage. Above all, the children must never bring any mud or dirt into the house. Esther had large ceramic white tiled floors, upholstered furniture, glass tables, doubled curtains with netting and tie backs, and small, neat pillows on the sofas. Her household had to look pristine, as if no children lived there at all. If there was a grease stain on the leather sofa, Judith Namala was in trouble. The maid was tasked with watching, hawk-like, for any stains that might appear on tables, sofas, and especially the white floor. Martha could play with her doll, but mostly she played with it outside, behind the house, in the small garden. It was the kind of household in which only the adults were allowed to sit on the sofa, while the children sat on a woven sisal mat next to the dinner table with the maid. On the mat, Martha and her toddler siblings' food and grease stains were more easily contained.

XXIV

Giddy on those days Martha was, when she could accompany Esther Nambi to the shopping mall, to the swimming pool, to the nail salon, or to church. The mother did not dote on her children. But being the eldest child, Martha got the starring role in her mother's tours. Martha did not mind going to the shopping mall, to the swimming pool, the nail salon, or to church, especially if she got herself a brand-new doll. Esther Nambi treated Martha as her understudy, even at the girl's tender age. At church, she knew how to correctly say out loud her full name to her mother's friend Jessica Nansubuga: *I am Martha Peace Nabirye Opolot.* At the swimming pool, she knew when not to swim too far out to the deep end. At the shopping mall, she knew how to hide her giddiness, and then scream out loud at home while unwrapping her hard plastic doll from its container.

XXV

Ntinda-Kiwatule 1999

Giddiness was a problem that her mother tried to cure. *Martha, you laugh too loud.* Esther Nambi yelled at the table. *Can't you see that I am reading?* or *Martha, girls do not laugh like hyenas.* If Martha was giddy, it was because she was a happy child. Born after the war that brought Yoweri Museveni to power, and amid the turbulence of the war of the Lord's Resistance Army in the north of the country, she was raised in relative quiet in the south, despite the reverberation of war in daily life. There were many displaced children begging along the high street of the capital city. More than once, Esther Nambi told the girl: *If you don't stop laughing, I will drop you off in the middle of town, so you can beg like those children with mucus running down their noses,* the children who had escaped the war in the north.

XXVI

It made sense to anyone, what was happening between mother and child. The mother raised her children, nursed them with her love and her hurt. With each *Don't climb the mango tree in the backyard, girls do not climb trees!* she showed both care and fear. It was that climbing trees came with its own set of problems. Girls did not climb trees, according to tradition. Martha could not avoid the judgement that would come her way. But when her mother's hurt showed, Esther Nambi said: *You do not know what it's like to live in a war. You do not know what war can do to someone. You do not know what war could do to your mother, your sister, or your brother.* These words haunted little Martha. Still a girl, Martha would learn later that war permeated her family and her country.

XXVII

Here is the girl-mother playing with her doll in the garden behind the Opolots' Ntinda-Kiwatule house. Here is the girl-mother plaiting her doll's flaxen white synthetic hair. Here is the girl-mother speaking to her doll, asking what she wants, whether she's hungry. Here is the girl-mother going to school and telling her fellow girl-mothers about her doll child, and here are those girl-mothers telling Martha about their doll children. Here is that verse in which the doll will be taken away, and the girl-mother will cry all day. Here is the girl-mother gazing into her doll's baby blue eyes. Again, again, and again.

XXVIII

Ntinda-Kiwatule 2005

The years went by, so to speak, and the girl-mother Martha became a young woman, Miss Nabirye Opolot. But one does not merely become a young woman, rather life teaches her how. *There was the matter of the girl*, as novelist Dambudzo Marechera wrote. The girl who was crying for her doll became a different kind of young woman: poised, purposeful, ready, responsible, even resentful. The matter of girlhood had been shaped by all of the larger-than-life figures around her, and womanhood had impressed upon Nabirye Opolot that these figures were made of clay. Once fired in a kiln, the clay stayed for centuries if not millennia. There was something ancient and unknowable about clay. But clay in the form of a pot was easy to break. Those larger-than-life figures were also fragile.

XXIX

This same girl-mother who nursed dolls, whose clothes were pressed by the maid, Judith Namala, was now old enough to iron her own clothes, brush her own shoes, and clean her bedroom. If the maid had been responsible for all the household chores, except on the few days when the madam Esther Nambi cooked a special meal for the family, the girl-mother-turned-young-woman Nabirye Opolot became a maid-in-waiting. It was a role that she hated. If Judith Namala did not peel green bananas, Nabirye Opolot did. If Judith Namala did not wash all the silk underwear and petticoats, Nabirye Opolot did. If the maid did not open the gate for Geoffrey Opolot, the young woman welcomed her father home. One late afternoon with the entire family in the house, Nabirye Opolot was given instructions, and she burst out: *Am I a slave?!* It shocked the madam to hear it.

XXX

Ntinda-Kiwatule 2005

A young woman, Nabirye Opolot, comes to an awareness of the oppression of the maid her family has kept over many years. The tender feeling of a young woman coming to terms with labor in the household, and what it might mean to be enslaved. The tender feeling of a young woman calling out her larger-than-life parents for enacting this system in their household. A young woman coming to grips with the state of affairs. A young woman calling out the powers that be. A young woman radicalized against her mother. A young woman coming to grips with oppression.

XXXI

The war within far exceeded the war without, before and after. It really was like that *house of hunger* Dambudzo Marechera described, in which every morsel of sanity was snatched from in the manner of hawks preying on little birds. The hatched chicks grew in a nest made of dried banana leaves, only the Creator protected them. We did not know how. They went to war one year, and left some goats behind. The older brother told his mother that when they returned from the tour, they would slaughter the goats and feast. This implies that they knew that their return was destined. But while at war the brothers were killed, each wounded from attack. Their bodies were left in broad daylight. To return is to go back to lay flat in the living room. So the saying goes: Do not leave your goats tied to a tree in the yard. Useless when war comes to your yard.

XXXII

Ntinda-Kiwatule 2007

The years went by and the earthen pots remained, so to speak. It is not a popular topic for a dissertation, the power struggle that ensues between a young woman and her mother in the home, but as the years pass, this earthen pot itself becomes a reminder. Time moves. Days move. Years move. Seasons change. But there are things that do not evolve, and one of them is the way that the madam Esther Nambi who runs the household looks at her child, no longer a child, but now a young woman by the name of Nabirye Opolot. And so, the years went by and the mother began to see this person in her house not as a child but as a rival woman.

XXXIII

Ntinda-Kiwatule 2007

The power struggle that ensues in the household is not merely about power. It is also a struggle over beauty, since beauty is one of the things that we fight for, that we establish, that we cherish, and that we guard jealously. The beauty that allows the mother Esther Nambi to maintain her place in the hierarchy of the household. The beauty into which a child Martha would become a novice. The beautyful that are born. The beautyful that are not yet born, as Ghanaian writer Ayi Kwei Armah would write. But what is guarded jealously? What is fought for? What is established? What could be born? What should be born? What had to be born?

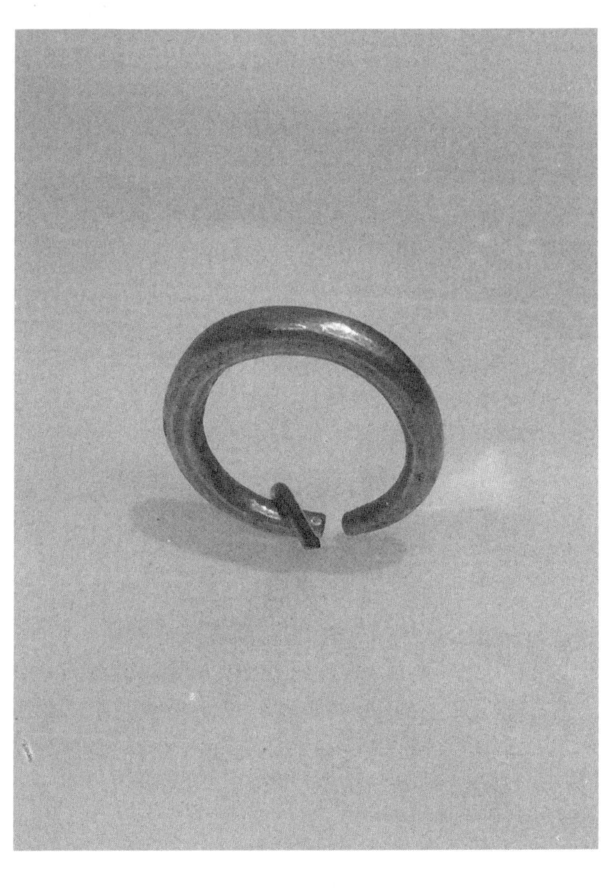

Nose Ring, attributed to Ethiopia, probably nineteenth century
Gold, 13⁄16 × 9⁄16 × 1⁄8 in.
The Metropolitan Museum of Art, New York

XXXIV

In a children's play, a musical interlude sets the scene before a Greek chorus recites: *dreams, dreams, and more dreams.* As a young person in the Greek chorus, you do not really know what dream, or which dream is being recited. How could one know what dream was invoked by this Greek chorus that intones *dream, dream, dream.* The line continues: *dreams which come and dreams which go.* But what the Greek chorus was reciting is this idea or this notion of a dream is comparable to beauty. Because how could one really know what was meant by it? How could one know which beauty? Indeed, was it even possible to have your own conception of beauty? As the saying goes, beauty is in the eye of the beholder. Or was that also truly just an opacity.

XXXV

Beauty is unknowable. Unknowable beauty. Unknowable beauty. Unknowable beauty. Unknowable beauty. Unknowable beauty. The unknown of the beautiful. The beautiful that could not be known. Undiscoverable beauty. Unmanageable beauty. Ungovernable beauty. *The beauty of a woman is no guarantee*, the Luganda saying goes. It cannot be agreed upon. It cannot be law. It cannot be formed by an act of parliament. It cannot be adjudicated. Beauty overwhelms. Beauty overwhelms. Beauty overwhelms. It overflows. It overflows. It overflows. It overflows. *The beauty of a woman is no guarantee*, the saying goes, and surely beauty remains ungovernable.

XXXVI

If Nabirye Opolot was given instruction in beauty, once a maid-in-waiting, she could not break the earthen pot herself–the pot was a symbol of the time shared between people. The earthen pot was broken through the tacit agreement of the household: That the maids were to become something other than themselves. That the children were to become something other than children. Once this unspoken agreement was set, the venom was loosed on (their) world in that idyllic house. Once the mother Esther Nambi became the madam, and hence no longer just the mother of her children, the maid Judith Namala drew the curtain and loosed this poisonous venom. And their world was thrown into a state of chaos and disarray.

XXXVII

If beauty awoke that sense of powerlessness, then the making of (their) world was bound to collapse. The girl, Nabirye Opolot who became the girl-mother, did not or could not establish herself in that role. Her motherhood, as the girl-mother, was assumed during girlhood. Once it came to building and making the household, placing the brick, organizing the house, establishing order within it, Nabirye Opolot could not be mother. Or perhaps more accurately, Nabirye Opolot could not be madam. She could not take this position. Powerlessness in the wake. Powerlessness was in her wake. Powerlessness was in her wake.

XXXVIII

Ntinda-Kiwatule 2002

That first season, when the mother Esther Nambi's attempts to discipline and punish fail. That first season of rebellion. That first season of talking back. That first season of storming out of the room without a care. That first season of: *You are not my mother.* This first season had come. And it was Nabirye Opolot's best season with seventeen touchdowns. It was a match between mother and daughter. It was the season of: *Cook like this, peel this green banana like this, wash this white shirt like so.* It was the season of: *This is how you dust the furniture, this is how you tie your headscarf.* It was that season. Nabirye Opolot's best season.

XXXIX

Ntinda-Kiwatule 1999

The green banana. The same green bananas that Martha saw out in the garden behind the house. The same green bananas that the mother Esther Nambi cared for as though her life depended on it. Those green bananas. So Martha would play in the garden, and when she got too excited, she would take every bit of wood or fiber she could find in the garden under her possession so that she could fashion these into a doll. And she was reprimanded. *Get away from my green bananas!*

XL

Ntinda-Kiwatule 1999

Many kept circumambulating around these green bananas. When Martha was finally allowed in the kitchen, where her mother Esther Nambi and her mother's help Judith Namala held court, she was asked to sit down on one of those beautifully woven multicolored sisal mats. She sat down without her legs showing, the way you are taught to do in Buganda. She was told to sit with a basket of green bananas, and to start peeling them. Martha heeded the instruction. She got to work on the peel. But she was cut by the knife, and her blood smeared all over the banana's sap. When she looked up, she saw Esther Nambi staring down at her with a smile. The sap formed balls of black sticky rubber. Martha had blood on her hands.

XLI

Ntinda-Kiwatule 1999

In this garden, when Esther Nambi had been home neither to look at nor to antagonize the girl, Martha went out to pick the dry bark of the banana plants. Her fellow girl-mothers at school had taught her how to use these dry barks to make magnificent dolls. The girl-mothers knew the composition of the dry bark and fiber doll, though no one quite knew how they had come to know it. The dolls had a refined architecture. They ranged in size, from an arm's length to nearly a meter. They had features: arms, legs, hair. The girl-mothers even knew what color of dry bark to use: darker colors to make the doll's dresses, warmer colors to make the doll's skin.

XLII

Manhattan 2000

You see them in Manhattan. All those Senegalese maids and the white babies they are nursing. All those Senegalese maids with the strollers walking up and down the avenues. Up and down the children's section of the library. All those black maids. You wonder about those children. All those white babies. All those white babies. Do they have a mother? To have a mother is something to begin with. What does it mean to have a mother? What does it mean to mother? And what would it mean to be without a mother? All the Senegalese women who left their homes and their children in order to nurse white babies in Manhattan.

XLIII

Ntinda-Kiwatule 1993

Did Martha have a mother? The mother is the first person to call you. Whatever name she gives you becomes the name you respond to. It doesn't matter if your name changes later on. If you become a different person, if you marry, or if you migrate and resettle in another land. You still recall the name your mother called you. And so, Esther Nambi called her daughter Martha. *Now her doll is ruined*, the madam said, *Martha will cry all day and disturb me!* It didn't matter whether her doll was tall or short. Whether the doll was made of fiber or bark or hard plastic. That did not matter. What mattered was that undulating voice that yelled at Martha while it calmed and held her. The voice that mattered.

XLIV

How did Martha make it out of that home alive? Here we arrive at the fact that Martha will someday become more than a girl-mother: She will become her own woman. Usually, in the common usage of these words, this meant that Martha would have to leave the home. What about the girl-mother who was raised by the voices in her head? Perhaps it was never about making it out, but rather about coming to terms. Even if coming to terms was coming to blows. It was never about surviving. It was the imminent presence of death. The dead looming over the home. Every home had its ancestral shrine and its welcomed ghosts that dined, drank, and ate.

XLVII

Ntinda-Kiwatule 2007

The mother Esther Nambi's attempt to discipline her child, and the child Martha's attempt to discipline her mother. Like Warsan Shire wrote, it was an act of teaching (her) mother how to give birth. *Shire's girl becomes a woman in spite of her mother.* Was it through ancestry and its ghosts? One wonders about the nature of motherhood and its relation to birth, but it is not always true motherhood is associated with ancestry, particularly in a society that emphasizes that the child inherits from the father, Geoffrey Opolot, and not the mother, Esther Nambi. This inheritance is further splintered along the lines of gender. It seems unlikely that the child inherited from the mother. What happened more often was that the child took after the father, and took the father's name. In the case of Martha, she became Martha Nabirye Opolot.

XLVIII

Ntinda-Kiwatule 1993

In the afternoons, after giving the baby Martha a bath and picking up the other child, Josiah, from kindergarten, Esther Nambi would sit in the drawing room and write. Often, she would write letters to family members in London and Stockholm, where it was said the largest population of Ugandans outside the country lived—other than Boston. Esther Nambi wrote to her sister who had moved with her young children to London in the early 1990s, at a time when the country was in the grips of political upheaval. The war in 1986 was shorter than the one before, in 1979, which deposed Idi Amin. Many had become displaced or gone into exile. The war had unleashed an atmosphere of fear.

Esther Nambi, like many of her contemporaries, got involved in the women's movement. She was a supporter of the Association of Women Lawyers, to which her friend Jessica Nansubuga belonged, particularly in their campaign against domestic and gender-based violence.

This, following the UN World Conference on Women of 1985 in Nairobi, where Hillary Clinton was shocked to learn that domestic violence was a norm for Third

World women. Like Burkina Faso president Thomas Sankara had described it, the lawyers were a group of bourgeois women whose fight for women's rights often extended only to literate and educated middle-class women like Esther Nambi—these made up the majority of their clientele, and indeed the majority of their court cases. Esther Nambi, who had attended Gayaza, a British colonial boarding school, had also attended university in the late 1980s under its gender diversity policy. But if gender diversity programs created more parity in the workforce, they did so mostly for elite and bourgeois women. Conversely, rural women like Judith Namala, her mother, and her grand-mother were all but forgotten by these policies. Esther Nambi sits in her drawing room. It is a hot and sunny day, and she sits in a chair by the window, watching the trees sway in her garden. In the letter she writes to her sister, she talks about the latest in women's fashion and makes a request for her sister to send her bags and shoes from Marks & Spencer. She's inspired by the latest fashions worn by Diana Windsor, Princess of Wales. She's writing the letter to her sister when she hears a sharp piercing sound coming from outside. Caught off-guard, she immediately stops, her heart racing as she starts to sweat. She waits for a few more seconds, frozen in what seems like suspended animation. Her forehead breaks out in pearls and pearls of sweat. She is still frozen when Judith Namala walks into the room. *What was that?* Esther Nambi asks, forgetting herself.

Before Judith Namala can respond, Esther Nambi focuses a wild piercing stare, her eyes glazed over and set ablaze with fear and awe.

The tension between rural and urban elite women played out like a soap opera in their household. Judith Namala, unwed and having left her child Subira in the care of her mother and grandmother in Masaka, had to look after and raise Esther Nambi's children in Kampala. Esther Nambi, literate and British-educated, benefited from gender diversity policies for her education, and became a housewife with three children. It seemed that the only real confrontation between rural and urban women had to do with matters of care: of the household, of the children, and of the husband. And very often, in spite of the many strides made by the local women's movement, that burden was hoisted like a parasite onto the rural women.

XLV

Sometimes she'd wake up before sunrise at 4 or 4:30 am. She'd go outside, opening the backdoor of the house, to begin digging in her garden. Esther Nambi was a modern woman with a degree in Business Administration from the Business School in Nakawa, but she was capable of tending to her garden. She planted green bananas and sweet yellow bananas, papayas, sweet potatoes, beans, yams, and cassava. She always said that if ever the war returned to Kampala as it had in the late 1970s and mid-1980s, she would have enough food in the garden to feed her entire family for weeks. Sometimes, at 4:30 or 5 am, just as the priests got up and rang the church bells and the imams made the call for prayer on the loudspeaker, Esther Nambi would tend to her garden. The neighbor, an older widow called Tereza, would tell her over the fence at noon that her green bananas looked very healthy, the tree's leaves having grown to about seven feet. You could see these tall, larger-than-life plants from the other side of the fence. Tereza warned Esther Nambi not to leave her green bananas too long on the plant because the monkeys and birds would eat them. The Baganda were known far and wide as a banana-cultivating people, and as such, even though their people had only occupied the southern part of the country, Uganda had been called a forest of banana plants. Tereza often heard Esther Nambi digging into the earth at that early morning hour. It was a sound like no other. The earth, when struck, sounded like a body–round and plentiful, like a jackfruit when it's ripe to eat. It was resonant, not hollow. Esther Nambi would dig and dig and dig, clawing out the weeds, planting new green banana shoots, and harvesting yams and cassava roots. Sometimes she went digging to fill the earth and prepare it for planting. Sometimes in her sleep she dreamed of new green banana flowers. The green banana flower, from which the fruit grew, was a large one. It was shaped like a heart and was probably the size as well. She dreamt at times that she was seeing her plantains flower and this gave her peace, knowing that her garden was capable of such marvelous returns.

XLVI

Masaka 1970s

It is hard to say what exactly was in Judith Namala's dreams. It is tempting to think that her dreams had a color, and that the color of her dreams was a deep purple, because this was the color of yams. Sometimes when the elephant ears of yams grew, they did not grow into a lime or clear green, but rather into a deep purple. She would watch the rain pour as a child, and stand under or go running around in it. When the rain dried, it would leave pearls of rainwater collected in the elephant ears. She enjoyed this and she would go and hide under the leaves, making them bend so that the pearls of collected rainwater would roll off the giant elephant ear leaves and pour onto her beautifully cornrowed hair. Her dreams were deep purple. Like elephant ears. Like banana bark once the plant had grown big enough to bear fruit the color of ripening coffee beans before they are taken off the plant stalks. In these deep purple dreams, she would see this girl with perfectly plated hair. That girl who enjoyed the rainy season, and that girl who played in the elephant ears of yams.

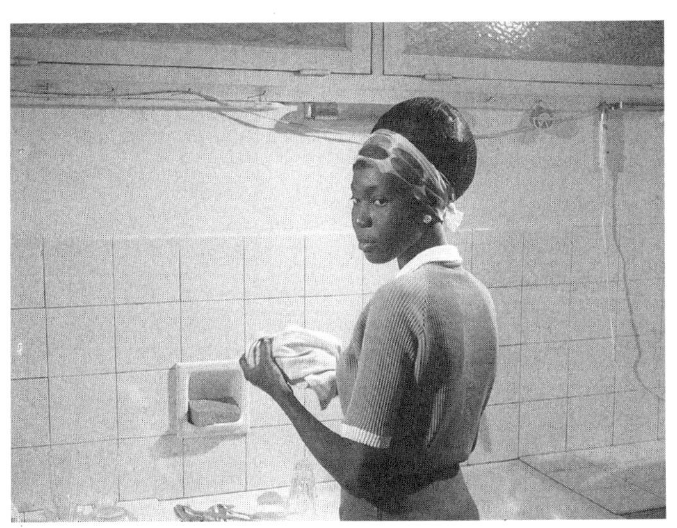

Diouana (Mbissine Thérèse Diop) in *La Noire de . . .*,
directed by Ousmane Sembène, 1966
Courtesy of Fimi Domireew

Acknowledgments

Judith Namala: A Novella came out of my interest in Ugandan popular music. The short lyrical stories of songs by Fred Sebatta, Dan Mugula, and Christopher Ssebadduka became the basis for each and every character in this novel. The approach to the novel is inspired by the late writer Binyavanga Wainaina, who told me more than a decade ago to write a novel in Luganda and translate it to English. I took the lyrics of Luganda songs and translated them obliquely into creative vignettes written in English. I maintained a direct Luganda-to-English translation of the song lyrics in a few places.

This work has benefited from correspondence with author Nakisanze Segawa, who read earlier versions of the text, made corrections to the Luganda-to-English translation, and corrected usage of Luganda words and expressions. I also thank the Center for Art, Research and Alliances team, including Rachel Valinsky and Manuela Moscoso, for publishing this book.

Thanks to Randy Kennedy, editor-in-chief of *Ursula* magazine, for publishing an earlier and shorter version of this text.

The text has gained from the following novels, short stories, essays, news reports, speeches, songs, and films: Fred Sebatta (featuring Harriet Sanyu), "Dole Yomwana" (1996) and "Nfisizawo Akadde" (2015) (I and II, pp. 11–14); Ousmane Sembène, *La Noire de* .... (1966) (II, p. 12); Mike Ssegawa, "Every maid is a reflection of her madam," *Daily Monitor* (November 27, 2014) (III, p. 15); Zukiswa Wanner, *The Madams* (2006) (IV, p. 16); *That's Life Mwattu!* (c. 1995) (VIII, p. 24–25); Serubiri Moses, "The Bad Blacks," *Chimurenga Chronic* (November 2013) (XIV, p. 36–37); Jennifer Nansubuga Makumbi, *A Girl Is a Body of Water* (2020), and Writivism Festival, Kampala, Uganda (June 17–21, 2015) (XV, p. 48); Robert Serumaga, *Return to the Shadows* (1969) (XV, p. 38); Toni Morrison, *Playing in the Dark: Whiteness and the Literary Imagination* (1992) (XX, p. 43); Dambudzo Marechera, *The House of Hunger* (1978) (XXVIII, p. 51; and XXXI, p. 54); Ayi Kwei Armah, *The Beautyful Ones Are Not Yet Born* (1968) (XXXIII, p. 56); Toni Morrison, *Sula* (1973) (XXXIV, p. 59); "5000 Proverbs," learnluganda.com (XXXV, p. 60); Jamaica Kincaid, "Girl" (1978) (XXXVIII, p. 63); Warsan Shire, *Teaching My Mother How to Give Birth* (2011) (XLVII, p. 70); Hillary Clinton, "Remarks to the U.N. 4th World Conference on Women Plenary Session," Beijing, China (September 5, 1995) (XLVIII, p. 71–73).

Finally, working from the Luganda language, which is at least nine centuries old, and possibly predates the English language in its current grammatical form, made me think about images that correlate to concepts of beauty and aesthetics in Luganda (and other African languages and cultures, including Swahili and Yoruba). This led me to consider works from the collections of African art in The Metropolitan Museum of Art as well as in the Brooklyn Museum in New York, where I live, that appear to be a century or more old, and which are used as proximate rather than literal references to aesthetic ideas in Luganda.

Judith Namala: A Novella

Cover: Asante, *Comb with Head, Sankofa Bird and Clenched Fist*, Ashanti Region, Ghana, late nineteenth/early twentieth century. Wood, 8 1/16 × 3 1/8 in. Brooklyn Museum, New York

Editor: Rachel Valinsky
Copy editor: Re'al Christian
Designers: Stoodio Santiago da Silva, Bárbara Acevedo Strange, Moritz Appich

Printer: KOPA, Lithuania
This book is typeset in Imprint URW and printed on Holmen Book and Olin Colors

Practice, vol. 1
ISBN: 978-1-954939-09-7
LCCN: 2025934715

Distributed worldwide by
ARTBOOK | D.A.P.
75 Broad Street, Suite 630
New York, NY 10004
orders@dapinc.com
www.artbook.com

Center for Art, Research and Alliances (CARA)
225 West 13th Street, New York, NY 10011
www.cara-nyc.org

CARA is an arts nonprofit, research center, and publisher that aims to expand public discourses and historical records to reflect art's abundant pasts, presents, and futures. Through initiatives including publishing, exhibitions, public programs, and fellowships, we seek to challenge dominant narratives and amplify the breadth of arts and culture.

Center for Art,
Research and Alliances